W9-DIN-228

Jupiter, Saturn, Uranus, and Neptune

By Gregory Vogt

Raintree Steck-Vaughn Publishers

A Harcourt Company

Austin · New York

www.steck-vaughn.com

OUR UNIVERSE

Published by Raintree Steck-Vaughn Publishers, an imprint of Steck-Vaughn Company.

Library of Congress Cataloging-in-Publication Data
Vogt, Gregory.
        Jupiter, Saturn, Uranus, and Neptune/by Gregory Vogt.
            p.cm. (Our universe)
        Includes index.
        ISBN 0-7398-3109-7
        1. Jupiter (Planet)--Juvenile literature. 2. Saturn (Planet)--Juvenile literature. 3. Uranus (Planet)--Juvenile literature. Neptune (Planet)--Juvenile literature. I. Title.

Printed in the United States of America
10 9 8 7 6 5 4 3 2 1 W 04 03 02 01 00

Produced by Compass Books

Photo Acknowledgments
E. Karkoschka (University of Arizona), 32; All photographs courtesy of NASA.

Content Consultant
David Jewitt
Professor of Astronomy
University of Hawaii Institute for Astronomy

Contents

Jupiter

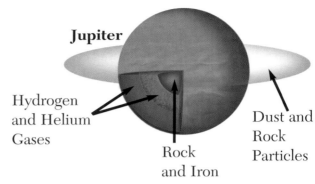

Hydrogen
and Helium
Gases

Dust and
Rock
Particles

Rock
and Iron

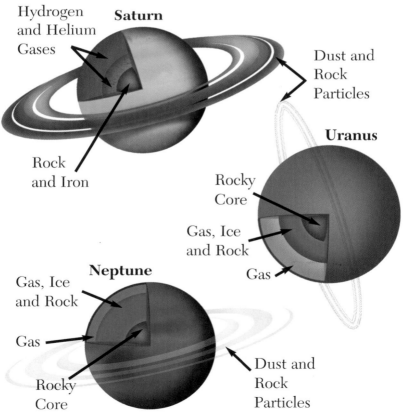

Hydrogen
and Helium
Gases

Saturn

Dust and
Rock
Particles

Uranus

Rock
and Iron

Rocky
Core

Gas, Ice
and Rock

Neptune

Gas, Ice
and Rock

Gas

Gas

Gas

Rocky
Core

Dust and
Rock
Particles

A Quick Look at the Gas Planets

What is a planet?
A planet is a large ball of gas or rock that circles a star.

How many planets are there?
There are nine known planets in our solar system. The planets circle a star called the Sun. Scientists believe there are more planets that circle other stars.

What are the gas planets?
The gas planets are four giant planets that orbit beyond Mars, far from the Sun. They are made mostly of gas.

What is the largest gas planet?
Jupiter is the largest gas planet. In fact, Jupiter is the largest planet in our solar system.

What are rings?
Each gas planet is surrounded by rings. The rings are made up of small pieces of rock, dust, and ice.

Which planet has the most rings?
Saturn has the most rings. It is surrounded by thousands of tiny rings that look like the grooves on a CD.

Which planet has the fewest rings?
Jupiter has the fewest rings. It only has three, faint rings.

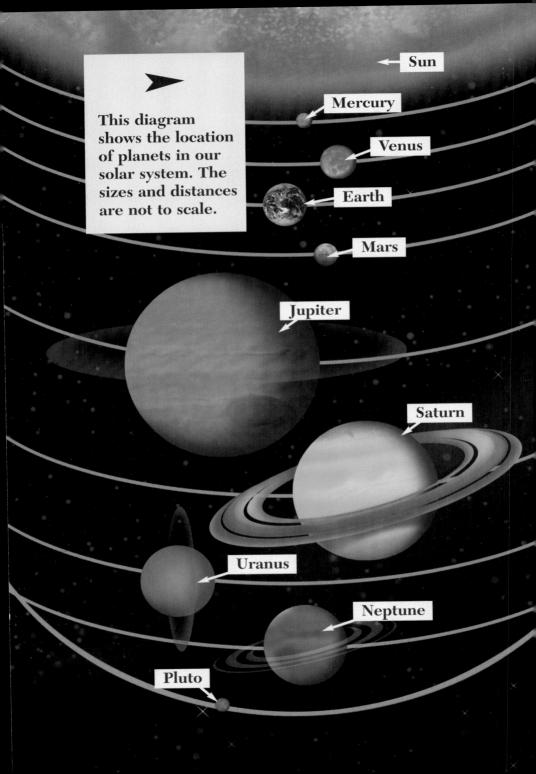

Sun

Mercury

Venus

This diagram shows the location of planets in our solar system. The sizes and distances are not to scale.

Earth

Mars

Jupiter

Saturn

Uranus

Neptune

Pluto

Planets in the Solar System

The Sun is a star. From deep in outer space, it looks like other stars. It is average in size and not very bright. But the Sun is different from other stars. Most stars occur in pairs. The Sun has no companion star. Many stars have no objects circling them. But the Sun has nine planets circling it. The planets travel around the Sun in paths called orbits.

The four planets closest to the Sun are small. These planets are Mercury, Venus, Earth, and Mars. Scientists call them the inner planets, or terrestrial planets. Terrestrial means made of earth or land. These planets are made mostly of rock.

Four other planets are made mostly of very cold gas. These planets are called the gas planets, or outer planets. Jupiter, Saturn, Uranus, and Neptune orbit in a set order far from the Sun. Beyond Neptune is the ninth planet, Pluto. It is made of rock and ice.

The Solar Nebula

The Sun and all the objects that circle it make up our solar system. Most scientists believe the solar system formed billions of years ago.

One idea is that the Sun and its planets formed in a large cloud of gas and dust called a nebula. A shock wave from an exploding star crashed into the nebula. This powerful wave of energy made the nebula collapse into a flat disk. The disk began to spin. The gas and dust in the nebula were pulled together by gravity. Gravity is a natural force that attracts objects to each other.

Most of the gas and dust fell to the center of the nebula and became the Sun. The gas got very hot. The hydrogen gas began to turn into helium. Energy from this process was released as light and heat.

The Sun's gravity pulled the rest of the gas and dust into a disklike cloud. The cloud orbited the Sun. Inside the cloud, clumps of dust formed. Heavier materials joined together near the middle of the cloud. Smaller clumps crashed into each other. They became larger clumps. Over millions of years, the clumps became the terrestrial planets.

Scientists believe planets and stars are forming in this nebula.

Lighter materials, such as gas and ice, formed clumps together farther away from the Sun. They grew larger and became the gas planets.

Planets are very different from stars. Stars give off light. But planets do not give off light of their own. They only reflect the light from the star they orbit, such as the Sun.

In some ways, the gas planets are similar. Each gas planet has many moons. Gas planets also have rings circling them. But the gas planets are also very different from each other.

People in ancient Rome named this planet Jupiter because it is the largest planet in the solar system. Jupiter was the Roman king of the gods.

Jupiter, the Striped Planet

Jupiter is the fifth planet from the Sun. It is an average of 483 million miles (780 million km) from the Sun. This is five times farther from the Sun than Earth is. Jupiter takes nearly 12 Earth years to orbit the Sun once because it is so far away.

Jupiter is the largest planet in the solar system. It is 88,850 miles (142,990 km) across. If Jupiter were hollow, all the other planets would fit inside it. Besides the Sun, Jupiter contains the most mass of the objects in the solar system. Mass is the amount of matter an object contains.

Seventeen moons orbit around Jupiter. The planet also has three very thin rings circling it. Dust and small pieces of rock make up most of the rings.

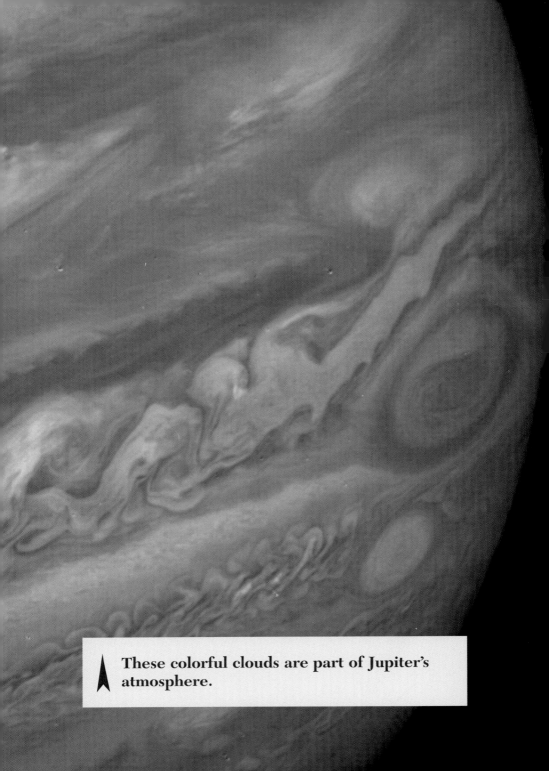

These colorful clouds are part of Jupiter's atmosphere.

Parts of Jupiter

The core, or the center of Jupiter, is made of rock and metal. A layer of mostly liquid hydrogen and helium surrounds the core. Jupiter has no solid surface because it is made mostly of gas.

Above the liquid gas is an atmosphere. An atmosphere is a layer of gases that surrounds an object in space. Jupiter's atmosphere is about 1,000 miles (1,609 km) thick. Large, colorful clouds form in the atmosphere. The clouds are so thick that astronomers cannot see the surface of the planet. Astronomers are scientists who study objects in space. They can only see the top of the clouds.

Three layers of clouds make up Jupiter's atmosphere. Each layer is a different color. The top layer is red. The middle layer is brown and white. The layer closest to the planet is blue.

Scientists are not sure what causes Jupiter's clouds to be so colorful. They think that the temperature in the atmosphere is so cold that the gases freeze. The different gases form crystals when they freeze. Scientists believe the colorful frozen crystals reflect light from the Sun. Each kind of gas crystal reflects a different colored light. This makes the clouds different colors.

Jupiter's Great Red Spot

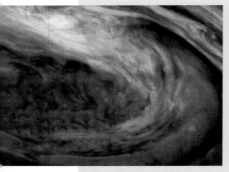

Astronomers first saw Jupiter's Great Red Spot about 300 years ago. The spot has changed its color and size over the years, but it has never disappeared. Scientists do not know what causes the spot's color. The spot is a storm in Jupiter's atmosphere that is two times larger than Earth. The storm has powerful, spinning winds that blow across the planet at 340 miles (547 km) per hour.

 The large whitish circles in Jupiter's atmosphere are huge hurricane-like storms.

Belts and Zones

Gases are always moving on Jupiter. Jupiter's core is so hot that it gives off more heat than the planet receives from the Sun. Because of this, warm gas is always rising from Jupiter's lower atmosphere. It cools in the upper atmosphere and sinks back down again. These rising and sinking gases form clouds and cause the weather on Jupiter.

All planets rotate, or spin, around an imaginary line called an axis. The ends of the axis are the north and south poles of a planet. Jupiter spins quickly on its axis. It rotates faster than any other planet. It completes one spin every 9.8 hours.

Jupiter's rotation and strong winds in the atmosphere stretch the clouds into bands. The bands are called belts and zones.

Red-orange belts are places where the cold gas is sinking back down into the lower atmosphere. These belts are made of poisonous gases. They look dark because of the frozen gas crystals inside them. Zones are places where warm gas has risen into the upper atmosphere. Zones are white.

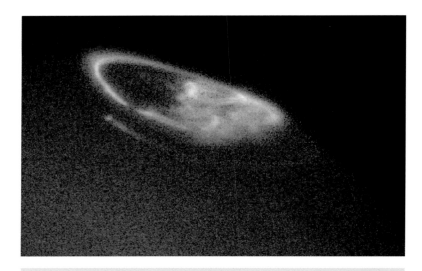

Auroras

Jupiter's magnetic field traps electrically charged particles from the Sun. Some of these particles glow when they come into contact with the gases in Jupiter's atmosphere. The glowing light from these particles is called an aurora. The Hubble Space Telescope took these pictures of auroras around Jupiter's North and South Poles.

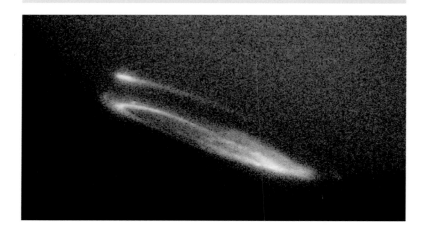

Magnetic Field

Jupiter has a magnetic field surrounding it. A magnetic field is an area around a planet that has the power to attract metals and objects with electrical charges. Jupiter's magnetic field is very strong. It stretches far out into space. It is 30 times larger than the planet.

The weight of Jupiter's outer layers presses down on the gas inside the planet. This squeezes the gas particles close together. The gas becomes like a thick liquid. The liquid gas moves inside Jupiter. The movement produces electricity. The electricity travels in currents inside the planet. Electric currents create Jupiter's magnetic field.

Jupiter's magnetic field traps some energy from the Sun. Because of this, Jupiter's magnetic field is full of deadly radiation. Radiation is energy that is sent out into space. Some types of radiation, such as X-rays and gamma rays, are harmful to humans.

Jupiter's magnetic field also traps other things. The solar wind is a stream of electrically charged particles from the Sun. Solar wind flows away from the Sun at thousands of miles per hour. Some particles from the solar wind get caught in Jupiter's magnetic field. The magnetic field guides particles toward Jupiter's North and South Poles.

NASA made this photograph from several photographs. It shows Jupiter and the four Galilean moons. The sizes and distances are not to scale.

Io

Europa

Jupiter

Ganymede

Callisto

Jupiter's Moons

Jupiter has 17 moons. Astronomers named each moon after characters from stories about the Roman god Jupiter.

Jupiter's moons are many different sizes. Some are about the size of Earth's Moon, and others are tiny. Jupiter's largest moon is Ganymede. At 3,274 miles (5,268 km) wide, Ganymede is the largest moon in the solar system. Ganymede is as large as the planet Mercury. One of Jupiter's smaller moons is Leda. Leda is only 6 miles (10 km) across.

Four of Jupiter's moons are very large. They are Ganymede, Callisto, Io, and Europa. Europa is the smallest of these moons. It is very bright because its icy surface reflects sunlight. Europa's icy surface has many cracks. Scientists think the cracks mean that a large ocean of water lies beneath the ice.

Io is the third-largest of Jupiter's moons. Io has many volcanoes that erupt, or blow out, the chemical sulfur. The sulfur falls back to the surface, giving the moon a yellow-orange color.

Ganymede and Callisto are made of rock and have icy surfaces. The ice on Ganymede is clean and grooved. The ice on Callisto is smooth and has dark material mixed in with it.

This planet was named after Saturn, the Roman god of the harvest.

Saturn, the Ringed Planet

Saturn is the sixth planet in the solar system. It orbits the Sun at an average distance of 885 million miles (1.4 billion km). It is the farthest planet that people can see from Earth without telescopes. Saturn is 19 times farther away from the Sun than Earth is. Because it is so far away, Saturn takes 29 and one-half Earth years to complete one orbit of the Sun.

Saturn is the second largest planet in the solar system. It is 75,000 miles (120,701 km) in diameter. Thousands of rings surround Saturn. The rings make Saturn look even larger than it really is.

Astronomers know of eighteen moons that orbit Saturn. Some even think Saturn may have more moons that have not yet been discovered.

Parts of Saturn

Rock, metal, and ice make up the core in the center of Saturn. The core is about the size of the planet Earth. The material that makes up the core is squeezed tightly together by Saturn's gravity. The core is hot and has great mass because a lot of material is squeezed into a small space. Saturn releases three times more heat energy into space than it receives from the Sun.

Thick layers of liquid hydrogen and helium surround the core. Above the liquid gas is an atmosphere of hydrogen gas and clouds. Scientists believe the clouds are made up of frozen crystals of gases and water.

Atmosphere

Fast-moving wind blows the clouds around Saturn. Wind circles the planet at a speed of more than 900 miles (1,448 km) per hour. This is three times stronger than a tornado on Earth.

An equator is an imaginary line around the middle of a planet. The equator divides a planet, or sphere, into northern or southern halves called hemispheres. A hemisphere is half of a sphere, or circle.

The equatorial jet is a strong wind that blows across Saturn's equator. Saturn's equatorial jet blows storms across the planet. Storms look like white swirls. The swirls of gas come from deep in the atmosphere. The swirls get larger over several months and then fade away.

The wind also blows the clouds into bands that circle the planet. Saturn's cloud zones are hard to see because a thick haze covers most of the cloud bands. Sunlight reacts with gases high in Saturn's atmosphere and makes the haze. This haze gives the planet a butterscotch color. Astronomers cannot see through the haze to Saturn's surface.

Cameras on a spacecraft took this close-up picture of Saturn's rings. A computer added the special colors.

Thousands of Rings

Nearly 400 years ago, the telescope was invented. Galileo Galilei was the first astronomer to look at Saturn with a telescope. He thought that Saturn looked like it had bumps. Galileo wrote that the bumps looked like ears. The telescope was too weak for Galileo to see that Saturn's bumps were rings.

Saturn's set of rings is 174,000 miles (280,026 km) across, but only about 500 feet (152 m) thick. From Earth, it appears that Saturn only has five rings. But spacecraft flying near Saturn took close-up pictures of the ring system. The pictures show that Saturn has thousands of small rings. The rings look like the grooves on a CD. From far away, the small rings blend together to look like large rings separated by small gaps.

Billions of pieces of dust, ice, and rock make up Saturn's rings. They range from tiny, pebble-sized pieces to large, bus-sized pieces. The planet's gravity pulls the pieces into rings that orbit the planet.

The view of Titan's surface is blocked by an orange haze in its atmosphere.

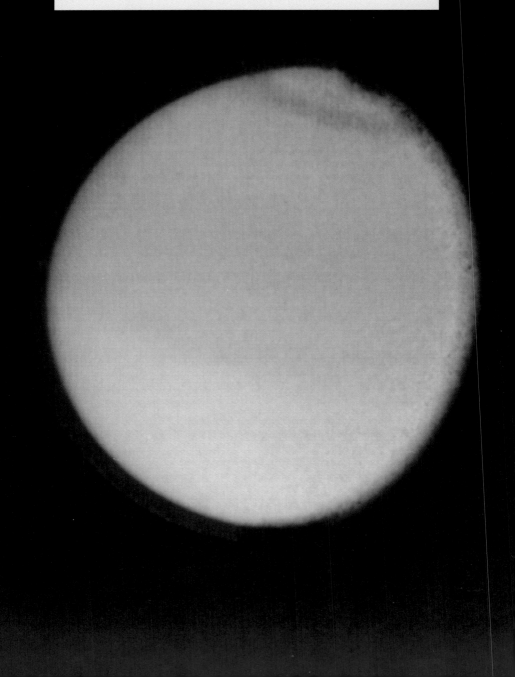

Saturn's Moons

Most of Saturn's 18 moons are very small. Some moons are just a few miles across. Several moons are shaped like large potatoes.

Pan is the closest moon to Saturn. It is 83,008 miles (133,583 km) from the planet and orbits near Saturn's rings. Pan is also Saturn's smallest moon. It is only 6 miles (10 km) across.

The farthest moon from Saturn is Phoebe. Its orbit is about 8 million miles (13 million km) away from Saturn. Phoebe is 68 miles (109 km) wide.

Titan is Saturn's largest moon and the second largest moon in the solar system. Titan is 3,200 miles (5,150 km) across. It orbits at an average distance of 760,000 miles (1,223,101 km) from Saturn.

Titan is one of the few moons in the solar system with an atmosphere. The gases in Titan's atmosphere are nitrogen and methane. A thick orange haze surrounds the moon. Astronomers cannot see through the haze to Titan's surface.

The temperature on Titan's surface is very cold. The temperature is low enough for the methane gas in the atmosphere to freeze into snow.

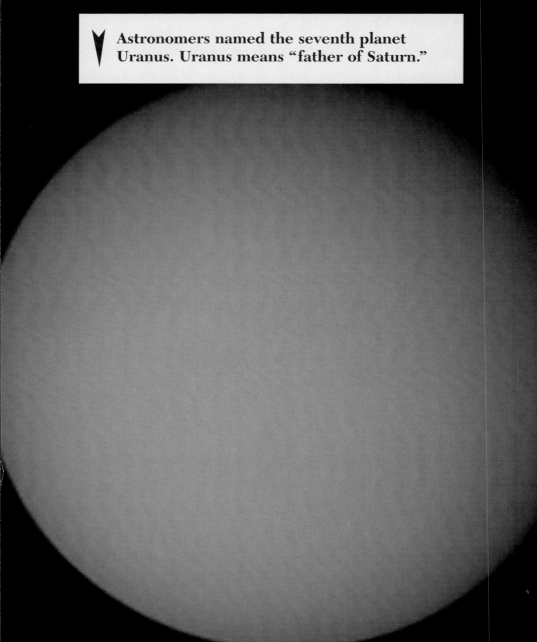

Astronomers named the seventh planet Uranus. Uranus means "father of Saturn."

Uranus, Sideways Planet

Beyond Saturn lies the seventh planet, Uranus. Uranus is the third largest planet in the solar system. It is 31,000 miles (49,890 km) in diameter.

Uranus travels around the Sun at an average distance of 1.7 billion miles (2.8 billion km). It is 19 times farther from the Sun than Earth is. Uranus takes 84 Earth years to orbit the Sun once.

Like Jupiter and Saturn, Uranus is a giant planet made mostly of gases. Like the other gas planets, Uranus does not have a solid surface.

Uranus has 21 known moons. That is the most known moons of any planet. Scientists believe there may even be more undiscovered moons orbiting Uranus.

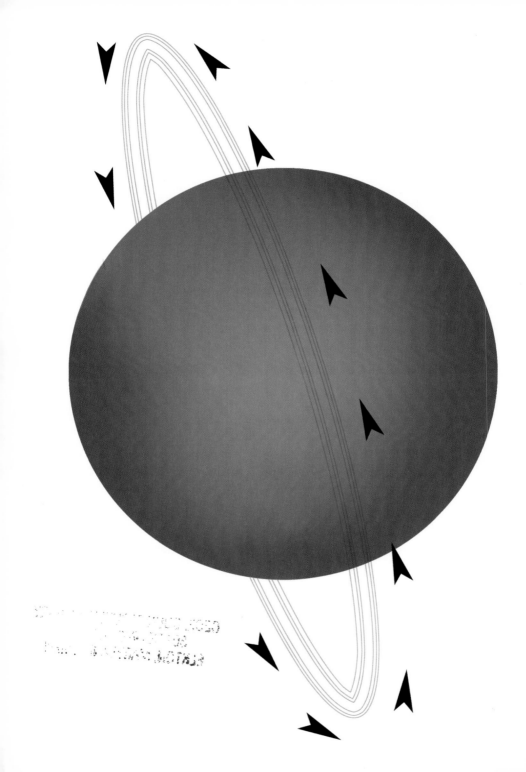

Rotation and Orbit

Uranus is different from other planets because it is tipped on its side. Most planets rotate upright like a top. But because of its sideways position, Uranus orbits like a top tipped on the side.

Scientists do not know why Uranus is tilted. Some scientists think it may have crashed into a huge planet-sized object when it was still forming. The crash may have tilted Uranus. This creates unusual conditions on Uranus.

Seasons are different on Uranus than on other planets. Each season lasts for about 21 years. Uranus's seasons last longer than the seasons of any other planet in the solar system.

For part of Uranus's orbit, its North Pole points toward the Sun. It is then light at the North Pole and dark at the South Pole. This causes summer at the North Pole and winter at the South Pole. During another part of the orbit, the South Pole points toward the Sun. It is then light at the South Pole and dark at the North Pole. This causes summer at the South Pole and winter at the North Pole.

◄ **This diagram shows how Uranus rotates.**

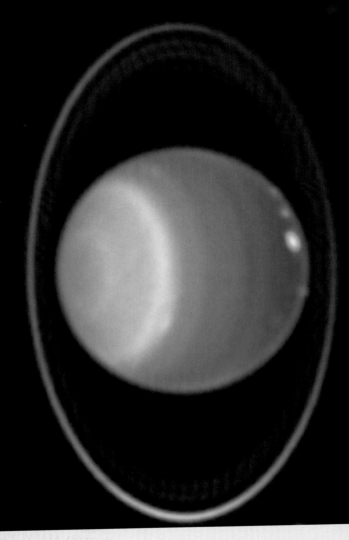

The colorful spots on Uranus are bright clouds from storms moving across the planet.

Parts of Uranus

Uranus has parts that are very similar to the other gas planets. Scientists believe a small core of rock and ice lies in the planet's center.

Scientists are not sure what the outer layers of Uranus are like. Some believe Uranus might have liquid oceans made of a mixture of water, methane, hydrogen, and helium. Other astronomers think the water and gas oceans are partly frozen.

Atmosphere

A thick atmosphere made of hydrogen, helium, and methane gases surrounds Uranus. The methane haze gives Uranus its blue-green color. It also makes it impossible to see any bands and storms in the planet's lower atmosphere.

At times, astronomers have seen some bright clouds in Uranus's upper atmosphere. Scientists believe the clouds are made of ammonia ice crystals. Ammonia is a combination of nitrogen and hydrogen.

Astronomers used the bright clouds to measure the wind speed on Uranus. They timed how long it took the bright clouds to move around the planet. They discovered that wind on Uranus blows at a speed of about 650 miles (1,046 km) per hour.

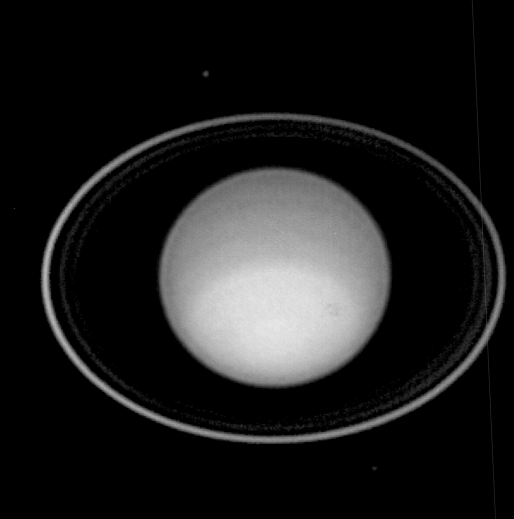

▲ **This picture from a powerful space telescope shows Uranus's ring system.**

Faint Rings

Eleven rings circle Uranus. The rings are from 25,000 miles (40,234 km) to 32,000 miles (51,499 km) away from the planet. Each thin ring is only a few miles wide. The rings sometimes make Uranus look like a bulls-eye on a target.

Uranus's rings are made of dark dust, rock, and ice boulders that do not reflect much light. This makes the rings hard to see from Earth.

Astronomers discovered Uranus's rings by chance. They were watching Uranus pass in front of a star. The astronomers wanted to study the starlight passing through Uranus's atmosphere. They hoped this might help them learn how thick the planet's atmosphere was.

As Uranus began passing in front of the star, the starlight seemed to blink off and on several times. Then it seemed to blink again the same number of times on the opposite side of the planet. The astronomers realized that the starlight blinked because rings blocked its light. Astronomers had discovered rings circling Uranus.

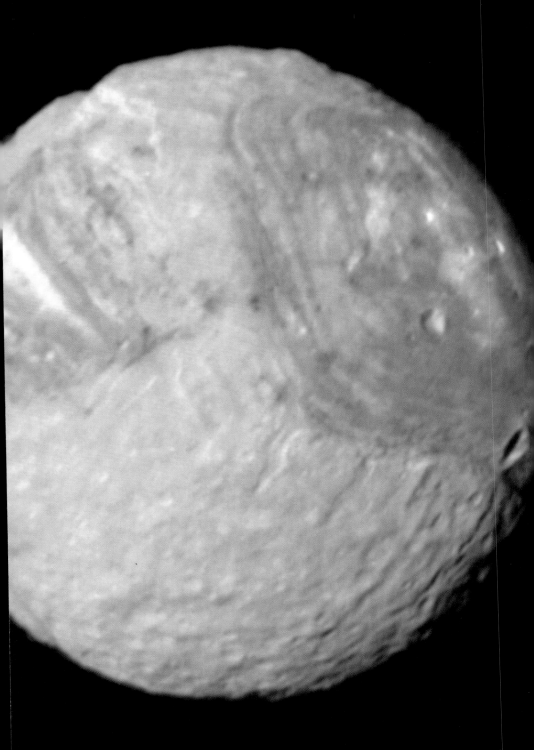

Many Moons

At this time, Uranus has more known moons than any other planet. Astronomers named most of the moons after characters in plays written by William Shakespeare.

The 21 moons of Uranus are all very small. The largest moon is Titania. It is 980 miles (1,578 km) across. The smallest moon, Cordelia, is about 16 miles (26 km) across.

Some of the moons are close to Uranus. Cordelia orbits only 30,000 miles (48,280 km) away from the planet. It takes only about eight hours to travel around Uranus. The moon called Sycorax orbits at a distance of 759,000 miles (1,221,492 km) from the planet. It takes three and one-half years to complete one orbit of Uranus.

Many of Uranus's moons are made of rock and ice. All have craters from meteorite impacts. Craters, cliffs, and cracks cover Miranda, Uranus's fifth largest moon. Its surface looks like a china plate that has been broken and sloppily glued back together again.

Miranda has many ridges and valleys crossing its surface.

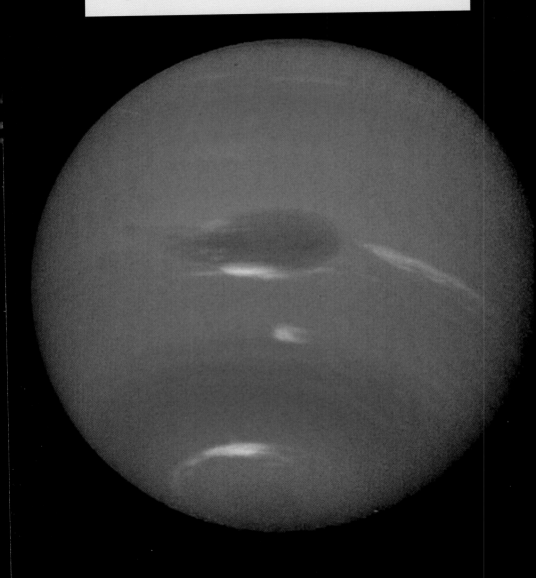

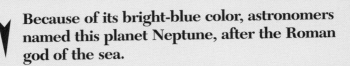
Because of its bright-blue color, astronomers named this planet Neptune, after the Roman god of the sea.

Neptune, the Blue Planet

Neptune is the eighth planet in the solar system. At about 30,775 miles (49,526 km) in diameter, it is the smallest of the gas planets. It rotates once on its axis about every 19 hours.

Neptune orbits an average of 2.8 billion miles (4.3 billion km) from the Sun. Because it is so far away, Neptune takes 165 Earth years to complete one orbit of the Sun. Neptune has not completed an orbit since it was discovered in 1846.

Neptune is the coldest of the gas planets. The temperature in its upper atmosphere is about –210° Fahrenheit (–350° C). Neptune is so dark and cold because it is too far away from the Sun to receive much light or heat.

This photo shows the Great Dark Spot on Neptune. It was a giant storm.

Parts of Neptune

Neptune is a great deal like Saturn. It has a rocky core. An inner layer of water surrounds the core. An outer layer of liquid hydrogen covers the watery layer. A thick atmosphere blankets the planet above its outer layer.

Atmosphere

Neptune has a thick atmosphere made of hydrogen and small amounts of helium and methane. A thick haze of methane gas surrounds the planet and makes it look blue.

Neptune is the windiest planet in the solar system. Heat from inside the planet rises toward the atmosphere. It flows through the atmosphere and creates great wind currents. Powerful gusts of wind blow more than 1,000 miles (1,609 km) per hour. They carry streams of frozen gases into the planet's cloud layers.

Faint bands of dark clouds circle Neptune. It also has white clouds made of frozen methane gas crystals. The planet's fierce winds may stretch the clouds until they are thousands of miles long. The winds also push the clouds across the planet, which quickly changes the shape of the clouds. Clouds may form and disappear again within several hours.

Neptune has an active atmosphere that creates violent weather. Large storms appear as dark spots in its atmosphere. Voyager probes took pictures of a storm the size of Earth called the Great Dark Spot. But the storm was not in new pictures taken in 1994. Scientists are not sure what happened to it. The storm may have stopped, or the atmosphere is covering it.

 This photo shows Triton orbiting Neptune.

Triton

Neptune has several faint rings and eight moons. Most of its moons are small. The largest moon is Triton. It is 1,680 miles (2,704 km) across. Triton orbits Neptune at a distance of 220,000 miles (354,056 km). The moon takes a little less than six days to orbit Neptune.

Triton is the coldest moon in the solar system. The temperature on its surface is –391° Fahrenheit (–235° C). Nitrogen and methane ice cover Triton's

Rings

Like all the giant gas planets, Neptune has a ring system. Several of Neptune's rings are faint. They range in size from about 30 miles (48 km) wide to 2,500 miles (4,023 km) wide. From Earth, the rings look broken because people can see only parts of the rings. Faint parts of the rings have less rock and ice than other parts. Rock and ice reflect light and make the rings look brighter. From closer, people can see the whole rings.

surface. The ice looks blue when it first freezes. It then turns red after it has been frozen awhile. The surface is also dotted with geysers. Geysers are holes in the ground through which hot liquids and gas shoot out. Frozen nitrogen, ice, and other materials explode from geysers on Triton. The material rises into the air and then falls to the surface, leaving streaks.

Triton is unusual because it is the only large moon with a backward orbit. It travels in the opposite direction of Neptune's rotation. Triton is slowly spiraling closer to Neptune because of its backward orbit. Neptune's gravity will pull Triton closer until it crashes into the planet. Scientists believe this process will take about 100 million years to complete.

▲ This is an artist's idea of what the *Cassini* spacecraft will look like as it lands on Titan.

Exploring the Gas Giants

Astronomers learn most about the gas giants by using spacecraft. The planets are too far away from Earth for scientists to see them clearly, even with telescopes. Scientists put cameras and other tools on the spacecraft. They use rockets to launch the spacecraft into space. The spacecraft fly near the planets and gather information about them. Radios on the spacecraft send the information to astronomers on Earth.

The Hubble Space Telescope is another tool for studying the gas giant planets. The large telescope is on a spacecraft that orbits Earth. The telescope has a clearer view of space than telescopes on Earth because it is outside of Earth's cloudy atmosphere. The Hubble Space Telescope has been used to take pictures of many planets.

Information from spacecraft helps scientists understand more about the gas giants and their moons. Scientists are sending more spacecraft to gather new information about Jupiter, Saturn, Uranus, and Neptune.

The *Cassini* spacecraft is on its way to the planet Saturn. It will arrive in 2004 and study Saturn and its moon Titan. A smaller spacecraft attached to *Cassini* will drop to the surface of Titan. It will send information and pictures back to Earth so that scientists can learn what Titan is like below its thick atmosphere.

Scientists are planning to send another spacecraft to study one of Jupiter's moons, Europa. The spacecraft will use instruments to measure the thickness of Europa's surface ice. Scientists hope to drop a robot submarine. It would melt its way through the surface ice and explore Europa's ocean. New missions will help scientists learn more about the giant gas planets.

Glossary

atmosphere (AT-muh-sfear)—a layer of gases that surrounds an object in space

axis (AK-sis)—an imaginary line through the middle of an object, around which that object spins

crater (KRAY-tur)—a bowl-shaped hole left when a meteorite strikes an object in space

geyser (GYE-zur)—a hole in the ground through which materials erupt, or blow out

magnetic field (mag-NE-tic FIELD)—an area surrounding an object that has the power to attract metals and electrically charged particles

meteorite (MEE-tee-ur-rite)—a space rock that crashes into the surface of another object in space

nebula (NEB-yoo-lah)—a huge cloud of gas and dust in space

orbit (OR-bit)—the path an object travels around another object in space

rotation (roh-TAY-shuhn)—the spinning of an object in space

solar system (SOH-lur SISS-tuhm)—the Sun and all the objects that orbit it

Internet Sites and Addresses

NASA for Kids
http://kids.msfc.nasa.gov

The Nine Planets
http://www.seds.org/nineplanets/nineplanets

Planets and Moons
http://wwwflag.wr.usgs.gov/USGSFlag/Space/wall/
    wall_txt.html

**Star Child: A Learning Center for
    Young Astronomers**
http://starchild.gsfc.nasa.gov/docs/StarChild/
    StarChild.html

NASA Headquarters
Washington, DC 20546-0001

The Planetary Society
65 North Catalina Avenue
Pasadena, CA 91106-2301

Index